You Saw Me S
and Other Short Plays

Six ten-minute plays performable by mixed or all-female casts

Includes the award-winning

"You Saw Me Standing Alone"

Leonie Thompson

DEDICATION

To David

CONTENTS

ACKNOWLEDGEMENTS

Thanks to David for his endless help and encouragement, to Richard for his advice and support, and to Jay for giving me my first opportunity to write.

And thanks, and much love to Mum, Dad, Em, Sam and Freya. X

YOU SAW ME STANDING ALONE

"Once in a blue moon wonderful things happen all at the right time, just by chance and it's a magical moment."

YOU SAW ME STANDING ALONE was one of the eight winning plays at the 2023 Ilkley Playhouse 8x8x8 festival whose theme was Once in a Blue Moon. It was first performed on April 13th 2023 at the Ilkley Playhouse with the following cast:

SAM   Flo Ameigh

AMANDA   Rachel Warren

CLAIRE   Heather Maude

Directed by   Darren Roberts

CHARACTERS

SAM, a teenager aged 17

AMANDA, a woman in her 60s

CLAIRE, a woman in her 60s

SCENE:

Black curtains and no set required. The lighting could reflect that this is set outside, with the actors standing on a vantage point, in late afternoon.

A teenager stands looking out to the audience. They have a notebook which they check very frequently. They are wearing headphones, and their music is playing so loudly that it can be heard by the audience. They regularly look through their binoculars, checking the horizon. The teenager is wearing baggy jeans and a large, black hoodie.

A woman enters. She walks over and stands a few metres from the teenager, also facing and looking out into the audience. Occasionally she uses her binoculars to look to the distance. The woman is in her 60s, is wearing a practical raincoat and walking shoes. She is crying, quietly.

They stand side-by-side and do not acknowledge each other for a short while. The music heard coming from the teenager's headphones is clearly of concern to the woman. Eventually she turns to them.

AMANDA Your music is very loud.

SAM What?

AMANDA Your music is very loud. You'll damage your hearing.

SAM Oh—okay. Do you think I should turn it off?

AMANDA Well, definitely turn it down.

SAM takes out their phone and turns off the music. They continue their previous behaviour.

Pause

AMANDA How long have you been waiting?

SAM Three hours.

AMANDA Oh—that's a long time.

SAM Not really. I waited five hours sixteen days ago to see a white linnet.

AMANDA You must be very patient.

SAM I am. (*Looking directly into the woman's face*). Why are you crying?

AMANDA (*a little taken aback by the directness of the question but remaining pleasant and calm*)

I was remembering. I have some special memories.

Beat

My partner died last year. And this place was special to us.

SAM Oh. Why did he die?

AMANDA She. She died because she had cancer.

SAM My mum had cancer. But she's okay now, They had to remove both of her breasts, but they did it to save her life. Why didn't they remove your partner's breasts?

AMANDA Her cancer wasn't in her breasts.

SAM Where was it?

AMANDA In her blood. She had a cancer called leukaemia.

SAM Yes—I know about that. When my mum had breast cancer, I made a list of all of the different cancers that people can get. I like lists.

AMANDA What other lists have you made?

SAM Oh—all sorts. (*Looking through their booklet*). The different types of pasta I have eaten. Names of the people on television I think should wear the colour green. All the things in my house which start with the same letter as I do.

AMANDA And what letter is that?

SAM "S". My name is Sam.

AMANDA Hello Sam. My name is Amanda.

SAM Hello.

AMANDA So that's why you are here now?

SAM Yes, last year I made a list of all of the birds which live or visit here and this year I'm making another list of all of those birds I have seen. It makes me feel happy when I see this year's list getting longer and longer—one day it might be as long as last year's!

AMANDA That's good.

SAM Why was this place special to you and your partner?

Pauses to reflect.

AMANDA We spent our first holiday together here, a long time ago. In those days society was not so tolerant of…people, women like us. The world was a different place. We had to pretend to our parents that we were staying at a friend's house with a large group of girls. But really it was just the two of us in a small bed and breakfast not far from here.

As she recounts her memories, a woman of a similar age stands up in the audience (it is important that her identity was unclear until that point) and makes her way serenely onto the stage. Neither **SAM** *nor* **AMANDA** *acknowledge her, but she walks around them in silence and stands behind Amanda. She is smiling kindly and looking out to the audience alongside the other two actors.*

The owner was very old and didn't say much. She never asked any questions although I think she probably understood about our…relationship. I can't remember her name anymore, but I can see her face now if I close my eyes. We were the only guests that week. Every day she would make us the most enormous, cooked breakfast and, just as we were about to leave the house, without a word, hand us some sandwiches wrapped up in greaseproof paper with a flask of instant coffee. We never asked for them, but we would thank her, put them in our backpacks and set off, armed with an Ordnance Survey map, to explore the local area. Sometimes we got lost—I am not very good with maps; I have to turn them upside down to work out which direction to go but we had such fun exploring. We laughed so much.

At the point at which Amanda mentions the map, she takes an old, well-worn OS map from out of her coat pocket, opens it and becomes muddled, turning it upside down. **CLAIRE** *gently and calmly takes it from her and slowly refolds the map as* **AMANDA** *continues with her story.* **AMANDA** *does not recognise* **CLAIRE***'s presence.*

You know, however much we had eaten for breakfast we were always ravenous by lunchtime—probably all the fresh air! Old "Mrs B-and-B" even loaned us a pair of binoculars one day so we could watch the birds from the cliff top and that's when we saw the grey osprey. It was all just by chance—we happened to be there at that time, an extremely rare visit to this shore, by an endangered bird, seen by us through borrowed binoculars, loaned to us for one day. But that's how life works, isn't it? Once in a blue moon wonderful things happen all at the right time, just by chance and it's a magical moment. Claire's pure joy when she spotted the osprey was just lovely, she actually jumped up and down with excitement… and that's when I knew I loved her.

CLAIRE, *who has an old-fashioned pair of binoculars around her neck, smiles, remembering, as the story of the sighting of the bird is told.*

We were together for forty-four years. Rarely a cross word and just so much love. My soulmate.

The women then face each other directly for the first time and smile. **CLAIRE** *gently hands the folded map back to* **AMANDA**. *They softly touch each other's faces.* **CLAIRE** *backs away and slowly walks off stage. Sam remains oblivious to* **CLAIRE** *but is still interested in* **AMANDA**'s *story.*

AMANDA *continues, a little confused but with new resolve to complete the story.*

Pause

And when Claire died, she made me promise that I would come back here next time if there ever was another sighting of a grey osprey and give her love to it in person. It seemed so unlikely that it would ever happen for ages, and I had no idea how to find out about rare bird sightings, but she had been so insistent. So, I joined a Facebook group and got "talking" to people who knew about these things. I actually met a couple of them in person last month when we had a local meet up and they are a really nice group of people. When I saw a post today about a possible sighting, I drove here straight away.

Pause

I think Claire was trying to give me a reason to keep going. She knew that I'd be a lost soul without her, and she was trying to make sure that I had something to do, some sort of purpose.

SAM She must have been a kind person.

AMANDA She was.

SAM I like kind people. I wish more people were kind. Some people are not kind.

AMANDA No, they are not.

SAM My mum's new boyfriend isn't kind.

AMANDA Isn't he?

SAM No. He calls me names.

AMANDA Oh dear.

SAM He calls me "weirdo". Because of my lists.

AMANDA That's not very nice.

SAM And he smells funny. I don't like the way he smells.

AMANDA Oh?

SAM He drinks beer. Lots of it. He smokes cigarettes too.

AMANDA Oh.

SAM Cigarettes cause cancer, don't they? I hope he gets cancer. I hope he dies.

Pause.

I know that isn't kind.

AMANDA I understand. How old are you, Sam?

SAM Seventeen. I am going to leave home one day. I live in a village five kilometres away. There is only one bus a day, but I like to walk. I am saving up my money from my Saturday job. I am going to travel. I am going to visit all of these countries. Do you want to see my list.

They proudly show their list.

AMANDA That's a great list, Sam.

SAM So, you are on Facebook? Old people like Facebook, don't they? I have a phone, but I like using paper and pencil to make my lists. I'm like an old person! *(Laughing at their own joke)*

AMANDA Yes! *(Laughing with them)*

SAM *(excited)* I'm going to join Facebook and we can become friends. So, you won't be so sad because I'll share my photos when I go travelling and you can like them. Do you know how to do that?

AMANDA *nods*

SAM And that way I will have at least one like. (*Noticing a bird in the sky and checking with binoculars).* Look. It's the grey osprey. The last time one was seen here was on 25th September 2017 and before that on 10th October 2011. The grey osprey doesn't visit here very often, does it? Today really is a special day, isn't it?

AMANDA It is!

SAM and **AMANDA** *watch the bird through their binoculars, their pleasure is plain to see.*

CLAIRE *returns to the stage, stands behind them and uses her binoculars to watch the bird too. She also smiles.*

Sharp blackout.

Music plays: "Blue Moon" by Julie London

DEPARTURE LOUNGE

An unlikely encounter between an international well-being influencer and one of her devout followers, reveals that their futures are increasingly difficult to predict.

DEPARTURE LOUNGE was selected by Constant Lark to be performed as part of their Twisted Tales festival.

CHARACTERS

GEMIMA, a female well-being influencer and "soul-healer", aged 18-40.

DAISY, a female of any age, but ideally younger than GEMIMA.

OFFICIAL, an adult of any age.

SCENE:

*The stage is set with a small desk up stage left
and several chairs in a row, facing the audience
down stage centre to right, resembling a waiting
room of some sort. On one of the chairs sits a
young woman who is filling in a questionnaire
attached to a clip board. She is dressed in
pyjamas and dressing gown, scruffy and
unkempt. She does not look well. Behind the
small desk, a person, wearing a smart office suit
and with an air of calm efficiency, is busy sorting
their paperwork.*

*A woman wheels a small suitcase through the
audience. She is very well dressed, wearing an
expensive looking, flowing dress, bright
jewellery, a wide brimmed hat and dark glasses.
She seems flustered and is clearly confused but
she speaks with confidence. She walks up the
steps to the stage which have been placed
centrally and approaches the official at the desk
who, sensing her irritation, makes her wait a
while longer.*

OFFICIAL (*with quiet authority*) Name?

GEMIMA Gemima Silverstone. Gemima with a
  G.

OFFICIAL Real name?

GEMIMA It is my real name. I got it changed by deed poll. (*Removing her sunglasses*). Don't you recognise me? Do you have Instagram?

OFFICIAL We don't have that sort of thing here. Occupation?

GEMIMA I'm a well-being influencer and soul therapist.

OFFICIAL (*searching the list on the clipboard*). I can't see that on the list.

GEMIMA Where exactly am I?

OFFICIAL The departure lounge. We need to decide where you are going. Next.

GEMIMA Going? I was flying to Rio. On my private jet.

OFFICIAL Yes.

GEMIMA I must have fallen asleep.

OFFICIAL Probably.

GEMIMA Is this a dream?

OFFICIAL Not exactly.

GEMIMA Sorry. I am very confused. Who is in charge here? I'd like to speak to your manager. Now!

OFFICIAL There are no managers here, madam. Just me.

GEMIMA But where is "here"?

OFFICIAL I think it probably best that you complete the self-assessment form. We seem to have run out of pencils. I will get you something to write with.

OFFICIAL *exits stage left.*

GEMIMA (*to the person completing the form*) Excuse me, do you know where we are?

DAISY (*looking up from her questionnaire*) Oh my goodness. Is that really you? Gemima Silverstone? Gem Stone Heals? I can't believe it, you're my absolute hero. I have always wanted to meet you! And now I have—that's so amazing! Wow, you don't know how much this means to me. I wish I had my phone so that I could have my selfie taken with you!

GEMIMA Well, I'm sure that I have mine. *(Starts to check her handbag which she finds is empty apart from a make-up mirror. She looks at it,* *confused).* I only have my mirror. And it's smashed to pieces. I can't see myself at all.

DAISY No, there aren't any phones here. No technology at all, I think. They don't seem to have made it through with us. I only have my handkerchief. I must have been holding it when I...

GEMIMA (*showing no interest*) No phones? Where on Earth are we?

DAISY Not really on Earth, as such.

GEMIMA Not on Earth?

DAISY Well, I think this is where people come when they have died.

GEMIMA I'm dead? What are you talking about? How can I be? How can we be dead? We are standing here talking!

DAISY I know that it is quite weird, but I think that's where we are. Somewhere that people go when it's being decided what happens next.

GEMIMA Oh my fucking God! I've died? I was just breaking into the South American market, my Instagram ratings have never been so high. Do you know that I had over 10 million followers last week? This is so shit! Why did I have to die now? What happened? How did I die?

DAISY I am not sure. I haven't been well enough to look at my phone for the last couple of days to follow the news or anything. I have been having palliative care, lots of sedation….

GEMIMA (*ignoring these comments*) Well, someone around here must know!

OFFICIAL *returns with a different form attached to a clipboard and a pencil, which are handed to* **GEMIMA**.

OFFICIAL Please complete this form, Madam. I will be back to collect it in a while. I advise honesty. The consequences for deceit could be…considerable.

GEMIMA I demand some explanation from you. Where the hell am I and what has happened?

OFFICIAL Madam, you are dead. We are deciding what happens next. But rest assured, you are not in hell. Yet. (*Smiling at their own joke*).

GEMIMA How did I die? I was on my way to launch my new range of chakra meditation beads and crystals in Rio. I had started recording series four of my Soul Healer podcasts, life was going so bloody well for me.

OFFICIAL I appreciate that death has proved inconvenient for you, Madam, but air travel has always come with a certain level of risk. The maintenance on your jet had been somewhat neglected and there was a weakness in the fuel line which led to a rather large explosion at 30,000 feet.

GEMIMA So, I didn't actually make it to Brazil?

OFFICIAL Well, strictly speaking, Madam, due to the manner of your death, some parts of you did actually make it to Brazil. But not all.

GEMIMA Oh my God! This is a disaster. Literally. I'm dead.

OFFICIAL Yes. Less than ideal, I agree, Madam. Now, please take a seat and fill in the questionnaire.

OFFICIAL (*to* **DAISY**) Are you finished?

DAISY Oh yes, thanks.

OFFICIAL (*taking her clipboard*) Thank you. I will now need to carry out a few checks. I will be back in a short while.
OFFICIAL e*xits stage left*.

GEMIMA (*sitting down next to* **DAISY** *and reading the questionnaire*) "In order to determine the most appropriate destination for you to spend the rest of eternity, we request that you answer the following questions as carefully and truthfully as possible. Question number one: "What words would you use to describe the sort of person you were?" (*Considering carefully*). That's not too difficult…caring, kind, spiritual, popular, successful, perhaps even inspirational? …that will do. Question number two: "What was the best thing you ever did whilst you were alive?" I assume they mean apart from helping tens of thousands of people to heal their souls and find inner peace?

DAISY What about your charity? The goat one?

GEMIMA Good point. That animal sanctuary has saved hundreds of adult pygmy goats from abandonment after they grew too big for goat yoga. Helped with the tax situation too, to be honest, but I won't mention that! Did you ever try goat yoga?

DAISY No, I didn't really have the energy for doing much.

GEMIMA That's a real shame. When I first posted videos of me doing that at the wellbeing retreat in Thailand, I could never have imagined the response I'd have from my followers. So many of them wanted to share in the joy of having baby goats climbing on them when they were doing their Sphinx pose, or whatever. But I think we had all underestimated the speed they grew at, despite their name, and then there were so many unwanted adult goats. I did feel a teeny bit responsible, so I set up the goat sanctuary in Cumbria. Cheap land, you see? (*Winking at* **DAISY**). Question number three: "Have you ever been responsible for someone else's death?" (*Throwing down the clipboard in disgust*). What sort of fucking question is that? I am a soul healer, a well-being influencer! How bloody dare they!

DAISY I got asked that too. I don't think they mean any harm or to offend you.

GEMIMA Well, I am offended! I am one of the country's most successful social media influencers and soul healers. I help people. I help the people who need it most. The sick, the vulnerable, those who have no one to turn to. And now I am dead. Just when my life was going so well, when my brand was going from strength to strength. I bloody hope that my death has been well reported and coverage has been good. It had better have been on the national news—or international, even—none of this local radio rubbish!

DAISY Oh, I am sure it would have been covered extensively. You were so well known. So famous all over the world!

GEMIMA (*reassured by this idea*) I am sure you are right. You know what? They say that there is no such thing as bad publicity, perhaps I have become even more of an icon now that I am dead? And everyone will remember me looking like this too—young and fresh-faced. No worrying about aging for me! That can't be a bad thing, can it?

DAISY Definitely not!

OFFICIAL *enters stage left.*

OFFICIAL Just to warn you, Miss, that your questionnaire has been checked and approved and I will be taking you to the Next Place in a couple of minutes. You need to finish yours, Madam. (*Peering over her shoulder*) Question three needs to be answered before you submit it.

(*Returns to the back desk to resume their paperwork*).

DAISY I think I will have to go soon.

GEMIMA Yes.

DAISY I can't tell you how wonderful it's been to actually meet you. I think you are amazing. You were amazing.

GEMIMA Thank you…sorry, what was your name?

DAISY Daisy.

GEMIMA (*very insincerely*) What a beautiful name. Just like you.

DAISY Well…

GEMIMA And Daisy, tell me, what did you do?

DAISY Oh, I was just a cleaner. And a carer. I cared for my aunt when she got ill.

GEMIMA Both such important jobs. I mean, I just couldn't do them—too…hands on for me. You must be a very special person.

DAISY Thank you. (*Becoming agitated*) Actually, I am a bit worried. I stole something once. It was just a lipstick, from Boots, when I was twelve, but it was a bad thing to do, wasn't it? Perhaps I will be punished now?

GEMIMA Well, it was a bad thing to do but…

DAISY It was a birthday present for my friend, you see?

GEMIMA I'm not sure if that's an excuse.

DAISY No, I know. (*Becoming upset*) I just wanted to be able to give her something.

GEMIMA Yes, well, it was only a lipstick.

   Silence

GEMIMA You said earlier that you had been ill. What was wrong?

DAISY I had cancer.

GEMIMA Oh dear, I am so sorry.

DAISY Cancer of the blood. Leukaemia.

GEMIMA And it wasn't treatable? Well, obviously.

DAISY Well, the doctor told me that I had a very good chance of survival. But that I would need chemotherapy. And I remembered what you had said in your podcasts…you know, how terrible those chemicals are for your body and how positive thinking and a careful selection of the right healing crystals could cure just about anything.

GEMIMA Yes.

DAISY So, I bought some from your website.

GEMIMA Oh. Which ones?

DAISY Clear quartz, obviously, and some rose quartz, you know to enhance its ability and some amethyst and, given my cancer, I decided to try some bloodstone too.

GEMIMA And what did you do with these?

DAISY Well, I kept them in a selenite bowl…one of your ones, actually, so that they would be cleansed and charged each day. I do love your merchandise! Or should I say "merch"?

GEMIMA Great.

DAISY And I did your online course…well, actually I subscribed to the bundle package.

Beat

But I must have done something wrong because I didn't get better. And now I'm here.

GEMIMA Yes.

Silence

And you refused medical treatment?

DAISY Of course! Like you said in your podcasts, all those terrible chemicals in your body are so damaging. And crystals have amazing healing powers.

GEMIMA Yes. Well…

OFFICIAL Miss, you need to come with me now.

DAISY Is it okay? Will I be okay. I mean, the lipstick?

OFFICIAL (*smiling kindly and gesturing towards the stage right exit*) Everyone is allowed a mistake. You were young.

DAISY (*reassured*) Okay. I had better go. It's been so wonderful to meet you. Thank you so much for everything.

GEMIMA (*awkwardly*) You are welcome.
As she leaves, **DAISY** *turns to wave
enthusiastically to* **GEMIMA** *who misses this as
she is already looking back to the questionnaire.*

DAISY *and* **OFFICIAL** *exit stage right.*

GEMIMA (*looking at the questionnaire and
reading slowly out loud*) Question three: "Have
you ever been responsible for someone else's
death?" Shit!

Sharp blackout.

*Music starts to play: "Hell is Round the Corner"
by Tricky and Martina Topley-Bird.*

HIRAETH

Two women strike up a conversation during their
journey on a bus and share some of their secrets and
stories.

CHARACTERS

GWEN, an older woman

MILENA, a younger woman of Serbian heritage

SCENE:

*Two women sit next to each other on a bus. The older woman, **GWEN**, sits next to the window and is carrying a large handbag and wearing a warm coat. The younger woman, **MILENA** has a laptop bag on her lap. She holds a mobile phone but isn't looking at it, instead she stares, wistfully into space. **GWEN** is looking out the window before she turns to **MILENA** and strikes up a conversation.*

GWEN I remember when this was all fields.

MILENA (*looking out of window, confused*) It is all fields now.

GWEN (*laughing*) Yes. I know. It's my little joke.

Pause.

It's what people say isn't it?

MILENA (*confused*) Oh. Okay.

GWEN I am going to the park with Toby and Arthur.

MILENA Sorry?

GWEN It's our weekly visit to the park.

MILENA Right.

GWEN Have you been to St Helen's Park?

MILENA No.

GWEN You really should go. They have just opened a new cafeteria—looks very smart. Beautiful rhododendrons. Not at this time of year. Obviously. But in June. Stunning. All sorts of colours.

MILENA Okay.

GWEN I like the purple ones best. Although purple isn't my favourite colour. To wear, I mean. Someone wrote a poem about an old lady wearing purple, didn't they? Who was that? I think I like pink better. Softer on the skin. Particularly when you get older. (*Fumbling in her handbag*) Do you want a humbug?

MILENA Sorry?

GWEN A humbug?

MILENA I don't know…?

GWEN Oh, it's a sweet. Minty and chewy. Don't see them so often now. I buy mine from Newson and Sons off the high street, it's an old-fashioned confectionary shop. All the sweets are displayed on shelves in big glass jars, like in the old days! There is too much choice really, but I like these best. They are rather nice. Try one.

MILENA Oh—okay. Thank you.

She offers the bag to **MILENA** *who takes one and eats it.*

GWEN Take two—keep one for later, if you want?

She offers the bag again and **MILENA** *politely takes another one which she holds awkwardly in her hand.*

GWEN I don't have anyone to share them with, so before I know it, they end up getting stuck to the paper bag and I have to throw them away, which is such a waste, I think. So, what do you think?

MILENA Yes, they are good. Thank you. Very tasty.

GWEN Is it alright to ask you where you are from?

MILENA Yes. Sure.

GWEN I mean, your accent is intriguing but difficult to place. I may be old, but I'm not a racist and I certainly did not vote for Brexit.

MILENA (smiling) I'm from Serbia.

GWEN How fabulous! And, may I add, I have never knowingly bought the Daily Mail. For a while, Gav across the road used to drop in his copy of the paper once he had finished reading it. I would wait until he was safely back across the road before announcing in my grandest voice, "Your toilet paper has been delivered, Sir!". We always laughed! The joke never got old. When poor old Gav moved into sheltered housing, the deliveries of the Daily Mail stopped. Terrible rag. Cryptic crossword was its only redeeming feature! Do you do crosswords?

MILENA Sometimes. But not cryptic ones.

GWEN They are so much easier if you have someone else to help you. So, Serbia? How exciting! That used to be part of Yugoslavia, didn't it?

MILENA Yes. A long time ago.

GWEN It may seem a long time ago to you, but I remember it well. Another neighbour, Jack, was in the army, he often spoke of the awful atrocities he had seen when he was serving out there. Hideous… (*she trails off awkwardly*).

Silence

MILENA Jenny Joseph

GWEN Sorry?

MILENA Warning

GWEN I'm sorry dear, I…

MILENA The poem, about the old woman wearing purple is called *Warning* and it is by Jenny Joseph,

> "When I am an old woman
> I shall wear purple,
> With a red hat that doesn't go,
> and doesn't suit me."

GWEN Yes! Oh well done! How clever! What do you think of it?

MILENA I like it. We studied it in college. It has a strong message. A good, positive message. About getting old.

GWEN Certainly could do with more of those. So, do you miss Serbia?

MILENA Yes, I do. I was due to go home to visit my sister for her birthday next month, but I can't afford the airfare anymore and knowing that I won't be seeing her or the rest of my family and the village where I grew up…it hurts so much. I seem to have a constant feeling of sadness at the moment, a sort of itchiness in my heart which I cannot scratch. I'm wondering if I am sick?

GWEN Ah, "Hiraeth".

Silence

Now, I am pretty sure that you won't have heard of that.

MILENA No.

GWEN Well, my mother would often talk to me about Hiraeth. It's a Welsh word that has no real English translation. It sort of means homesickness. A deep longing for somewhere, especially your home. A sort of pull on your heart that gives you the feeling that you are missing something intensely.

MILENA Yes—that's what it is. That's how it feels. At least I know what's wrong with me now.

GWEN Hmm. You said you can't afford the airfare anymore—has something happened?

MILENA Well, my boyfriend is trying to set up a business and it's difficult at the moment. Things aren't really working out.

GWEN No?

MILENA It's not his fault—but everything is so…tricky. Money.

GWEN Yes.

MILENA So, I gave him the money I was saving for the trip back to Serbia this summer.

GWEN That was very generous of you. I hope he appreciated that.

MILENA Oh, he did.

Silence

Well. I think he did.

GWEN So, what is his business then?

MILENA He's a mechanic. He's really good with cars. But he got in with a wrong lot and bought some spare parts from a man who turned out to be very bad. He owed him money for a while and the man threatened him.

GWEN Sounds very nasty.

MILENA He knew I had some savings from my
weekend job to visit Niki, my sister, and he
asked for them and I gave them to him. I didn't
want him to get hurt.

GWEN Lucky for him that you had savings and
are kind enough to help him out.

MILENA Yes. It isn't the first time it has
happened to be honest. He often seems to get
into trouble, with money. I try to warn him, but
he doesn't listen.

GWEN I am sorry if I'm speaking out of turn here,
my dear, but at my age I feel that wasting time
on subtleties and niceties isn't necessary or wise.
It sounds very much that your boyfriend falls
into the category of takers, whilst you are clearly
a giver. And that may not be a good thing.

MILENA What do you mean?

GWEN Well, over many years I have realised that
people fall into two categories—givers or
takers—financially or emotionally or whatever. I
think that you, my dear, fall into the giver
category. Now, if your boyfriend falls into the
taker category, then I have to say that could be
very problematic for the future. You see, you are

willing to give to him—money, time, emotional energy and he will just take those things, regardless of how much hurt or damage that may cause you. He probably won't even realise or notice this; it's just part of who he is.

MILENA Well, it does feel a bit like that sometimes.

GWEN I was lucky that I ended up marrying another giver. So, our main problem was that both of us desperately wanted to please the other, to the point that we almost forgot what we wanted ourselves and tried to second guess what the other one wanted—sometimes incorrectly. I remember ordering a lemon meringue pie for dessert once, only because I thought he liked it, just in case he wanted to have some of mine. Turned out he didn't like it any more than I did—we ended up leaving it untouched. I remember the waiter was seriously confused! (*Laughing*)

MILENA I will think about this. Thank you. Who are Toby and Arthur?

GWEN Oh, two of my dearest beings in the world.

MILENA And you are walking in the park with them? Where will you meet them?

GWEN Oh, I have them here, in my bag.

MILENA Sorry?

GWEN Don't think badly of me, but I have them here in my bag.

MILENA Are they animals?

GWEN (*Laughing*) No! Well, one of them was. Once.

MILENA I'm sorry?

GWEN I know this sounds odd, but they are, sorry were, my husband and pet dog. My husband was called Toby, which we always thought sounded like a dog's name, so when we got our pet Labrador, we thought we should give him a human name, you know, to add to the joke. So, we called him Arthur.

MILENA I'm confused.

GWEN (*Laughing*) That was the idea! They both passed on two years ago within a week of each other, can you believe it? Toby died first and then Arthur, who was his dog really, seemed to just give up. He went to sleep on the bed as he always did, a terrible habit, I know—I wasn't proud of that—but I woke up to find him with his head on the pillow, on Toby's pillow, stone dead. He looked so human lying there that it did make me smile. It was if he was in on the joke, you know? But to lose them both within a week was… very difficult.

MILENA Oh, I'm so sorry. That must have been so awful.

GWEN It was. It was a horrible time. Shitty some might say. Not me, because I don't swear!

MILENA No!

GWEN Anyway, after they had both been cremated, I decided to take some of each of their ashes, put them into this little box so they can both be with me all of the time. You probably think I'm a little bit mad and perhaps I am, but it helps me to cope, you know? Because I miss them both so much.

She takes a small box out her bag and shows it to **MILENA**.

MILENA I'm sure.

Beat

And I don't think you are mad.

GWEN Oh, here we are, it's the stop for the park. Where do you get off?

MILENA Well, I was just going to the library to use their Wi-Fi, but I fancy a walk. Perhaps I could join you for a stroll around the park? As long as Toby and Arthur don't mind?

GWEN Oh, I am sure that they will love to have somebody else joining us in our walk today. Perhaps we could have a coffee and a cake in the café? My treat!

MILENA That sounds very nice.

Both women gather their belongings, **MILENA** *pops the second humbug in her mouth, and they exit together.*

BUCKET LIST

Two old acquaintances meet and discuss old times.

CHARACTERS

MRS BUCKINGHAM, a retired PE teacher

KIM, a middle-aged woman

SCENE:

A woman lies on the beach she has been sleeping after a swim in the sea. She wears a white swimming costume with a light-coloured cotton shirt over the top. She has a beach bag, whose contents have spilt out onto a white towel. To her right is a flask of hot drink. Another younger woman sits very close, next to her, she is fully dressed.

KIM (*noticing that* **MRS B** *has just woken*) It's a beautiful beach, isn't it?

MRS B (*surprised at the presence of* **KIM** *sitting very close by*) Yes.

KIM Not a soul on it apart from us.

MRS B *(still confused)* No.

KIM All this space.

MRS B Yes.

KIM I really don't understand why all those holiday makers trudge down to Cornwall year after year. I mean, it's a lovely place, but really, is it worth the effort? Stuck in traffic for hours on end. The M4, just one long, very tedious carpark. Then being ripped off when they eventually get there and fighting for beach space with half of Surrey vying for the top spots. Terrifying seagulls too. Really vicious buggers! No, they can keep that!

Pause

Don't you agree?

MRS B Yes. Look, sorry…..

KIM Nice nap?

MRS B Well, yes…..

KIM I admire that!

MRS B What?

KIM I admire you being able to go to sleep on a beach.

MRS B Really?

KIM I couldn't relax enough to sleep anywhere outdoors. With others around. Having to trust others not to take advantage. I'd feel vulnerable.

Silence.

But I guess you aren't the sort to feel vulnerable?!

MRS B Not really. (*She takes her vacuum flasks and proceeds to drink her coffee during the following conversation*)

KIM You've been here every day this week so far, haven't you?

MRS B Yes. How do you…

KIM (*ignoring her question*) Every day you've been for an invigorating swim for half an hour or so, and then had a nice afternoon nap on the beach. I've seen you. Have to say that you are a very strong swimmer for someone of your age.

MRS B Look, I don't know who you are, but I'm finding this conversation and your behaviour a bit weird to be honest.

KIM Weird?

MRS B Yes!

KIM Is it making you feel uncomfortable?

MRS B Well…

KIM I'm sorry. It's not nice to be made to feel uncomfortable, is it? I wouldn't want you to have to experience that.

Beat

How's your coffee?

MRS B It's fine, thank you. How do you know it's coffee?

KIM Just a guess. I don't drink coffee. People say that coffee smells better than it tastes, and I think it even smells rank. Is it okay?

MRS B Yes. Why wouldn't it…

KIM (*interrupting*) The trouble with these remote beaches is that they lack facilities, don't they? I mean no toilets, or showers or places to eat.

MRS B (*sarcastically*) Perhaps that's why they are so peaceful?

KIM Do you think so? People just can't be bothered to make the effort with walking so far, carrying their stuff. What is it, 45 minutes or so?! Through the village, along the beach path, across the rocks. Quite a drag! They'd rather sit on a beach rammed with people than get off their lazy backsides and find these beautiful spots.

Silence

MRS B We have a whole beach and you've chosen to sit right next to me. Can I ask you why?

KIM Because I wanted to talk to you and I find it's so much easier to do that close to someone rather than shouting across the bay.

MRS B What do you want to talk about?

KIM Things.

MRS B What sort of things?

KIM Behaviour.

MRS B Behaviour?

KIM Past behaviour. To be more accurate, your past behaviour.

MRS B (*starting to gather her few things*) Look, I've had enough of your stupid games. Tell me what is going on.

KIM Funny that you should mention games.

MRS B Why?

KIM That's a name that I couldn't ever understand. At school. Games. Sounds like a fun lesson, doesn't it? When actually it was anything but fun for some of us!

MRS B Oh God. I see what's happening now. Are you some disgruntled ex-student of mine who I told off once in a PE lesson? Did I upset you?

KIM You know, when I heard you ordering your drink at the bar in the White Lion a couple of nights ago, I recognised it straight way. Honestly, I could barely breathe. Suddenly, my heart was beating in my head and the blood was rushing through my ears. My mouth went dry, and I thought I was going to be sick. Rather an extreme reaction, wouldn't you say?! But there again not all that surprising, given that yours was the voice that I feared more than any other during my early years at school.

MRS B Look, clearly you are in need of some sort of therapy or counselling or whatever. School was a very long time ago and you need to move on now. That time has passed.

KIM You have a point but when I heard your voice, Mrs Buckingham, I thought. Bloody hell! What's that nasty old b—what's she doing here? Well, I got interested and I started to keep an eye on you. I'd take a stroll to this beach each day, watch you swim, and sleep and I started to think.

Beat

No, Mr Buckingham, I notice. Travelling alone?

MRS B No, he passed away a couple of years ago. Not that it's any of your bloody business.

KIM Probably not.

Beat

Yes, I started to think. To remember.

MRS B Remember what exactly?

KIM Things. I wonder, do you remember what you used to do to us girls in that winter term of our first year at St Jude's? I remember. You'd make us take off our clothes and run the cross country in our underwear. Wouldn't even allow us to wear T-shirts or shorts. Was that even legal? How did you get away with it? However bitter the weather was. Do you remember that? I can see you now. You'd have that dark green anorak zipped up warm around you and you'd cradle a hot mug of coffee in both hands, and you'd shout at us as we ran around the rec. Call us names. Nasty names. I can feel that freezing air burning my lungs. And the slowest runner would have to stand outside in the cold for an extra three minutes—"cooling off"—as a punishment. It was always poor Jessie Hobbs because she was very overweight, and you'd tell her that her whale blubber should be keeping her warm any way. Once I tried to run slower than her to save her from the ordeal, but you got wind of my scheme and we both ended up "cooling off", standing outside. And then one week she wet herself. The poor girl was so cold that she couldn't control her bladder anymore. Tears of shame running down her face as the urine trickled down her leg, steaming as it flowed. And you let all the class know and humiliated the poor girl further by calling her Miss Pissy-Pants from thereafter.

Silence.

MRS B They were different times.

KIM But do you remember?

MRS B I taught so many students.

KIM But do you remember her? Jessie?

MRS B Vaguely, perhaps.

Pause.

What happened to her?

KIM She became anorexic in the sixth form. Had quite a successful modelling career for a couple of years and then died of multiple organ failure in her mid-twenties. Really tragic.

MRS B I'm sorry.

KIM Are you?

MRS B Yes. Of course. As I say, they were different times. We thought it was a good thing to be hard on children. To toughen them up, you know?

KIM No snowflakes back then, eh?

MRS B Exactly.

KIM No—just scared, miserable children at the mercy of bullying adults.

MRS B Look, I've had enough of this! What is the point of this?

KIM (*ignoring her*) A white swimsuit? Brave choice. My mother always warned against wearing white—she said that people could see your pubes when it got wet. Can you?

MRS B (*looking down*) I don't think so?!?

KIM Have you ever had an angiogram?

MRS B A what?

KIM Oh sorry—I forgot. PE teacher. Keep it simple. It's a medical procedure where they put a dye into your blood and give you a body scan to check the state of your cardiac blood vessels. I had one done last month. I'd been having some pains, you know? Anyway, turns out that, despite giving up bacon sandwiches a good while back, some of my blood vessels are starting to look narrower than they should. Furring up like the pipes of an old boiler.

MRS B I'm sorry to hear that.

KIM Thank you. The thing is, the doctors aren't all that surprised or concerned. It seems that most people of my age are probably in the same situation but just don't know about it. I'm going back next week to discuss the plan of action. But it got me thinking, we are all dying aren't we? I mean, every day we get closer to our day of death.

MRS B Well… I suppose so.

KIM And then I started to think about bucket lists. You know? You do know what they are?

MRS B Yes, of course. Things you want to do before you kick the bucket.

KIM That's the one. What's on yours?

MRS B Sorry?

KIM What's on your bucket list?

Mrs B: I don't know really.

KIM Come on. Have a think. It's fun.

MRS B Well, I don't know.

KIM (*forcefully*) Think!

MRS B Well…okay…I'd like to go to Las Vegas.

KIM Really? Las Vegas?! I can't think of anywhere worse! Conspicuous wealth, the excesses of human consumption—I'd hate that!!

MRS B Well, it's a good job I wouldn't be taking you with me on my hypothetical, non-existent trip.

KIM Could you afford that, on your teacher's pension? I'm assuming you are retired.

MRS B Yes. I retired early actually.

KIM Really? Any particular reason?

MRS B I wasn't well. Work related stress. I… had a sort of breakdown.

KIM Really? How ironic. I suppose that's some sort of karma! I mean, you caused overwhelming stress for your students and then you experience the same. Karma definitely.

MRS B Well…

KIM So, something on my bucket list was to take all opportunities. Particularly to take opportunities to get my own back on people who have pissed me off. A sort of revenge bucket list.

MRS B Oh, I see. So, this is where you kill me, on a secluded Welsh beach?

Silence

KIM (*smiling*) Of course not. I'm not a murderer. I spent my life working as a librarian. How would I kill you? Smash your skull open with a particularly weighty, hardback edition of *War*

and Peace? No, I don't want to kill you nor,
more importantly, do I want to spend the rest of
my life in prison.

MRS B So, what then?

KIM No, I've decided to take a more creative but
satisfying approach to revenge. So, for instance,
when I found out my ex-husband was having an
affair with our next-door neighbour, I left it for a
while. He had no clue that I knew. We were on
holiday, and it was our wedding anniversary, so I
invited him out for a romantic meal at a
Michelin-starred restaurant. I offered to drive
and told him that, at last, I had got lucky with my
scratch cards, and it was on me. He couldn't
believe his luck! We ordered the most expensive
meals, and I encouraged him to choose his
favourite vintage wine. Halfway through, I made
my excuses and slipped out to the Ladies, left by
the staff door, drove back to our holiday cottage,
packed and went home. I had taken his phone
and wallet out of his pocket before we set off, so
he had no way of paying the bill. I am hoping
that he ended up doing a lot of washing up that
evening to pay the debt, given the fact that the
lazy sod rarely went anywhere near the kitchen
in all our decades of marriage. The silly tart next
door may have been surprised to see her over-
made-up mug on the Missing Pet style posters all
over town. "Have you seen this Bitch? Warning:

approach with caution—has been known to steal husbands". One hundred posters—on every lamppost, billboard and empty wall in the neighbourhood. Perfect. *(Enjoying the moment)* And then we have you.

MRS B So, what hilarious revenge do you have planned for me then?

KIM Well, given your treatment of poor Jessie, I thought it would have to be some sort of toilet-related humiliation. Have you heard of bisacodyl? Well, of course you haven't. You are—sorry, *were*—a PE teacher. It's a laxative. A rapidly acting one. Easily added to your flask as you so trustingly caught your 40 winks. *(Checks watch)* In a couple of minutes, the contents of your bowels are going to be expelled rapidly and uncontrollably from your body. I'm surprised you couldn't taste it in your coffee— clearly not, as you drank it all down. Quite a large dose! *(Jumping up)* I'd love to hang around to witness this, but I think I'll give it a miss. *(Starting to exit the stage)* Enjoy the long walk home, Mrs Buckingham. Perhaps choose a brown swimsuit next time, eh?

KIM *leaves as* **MRS B** *looks on perplexed.*

Sharp blackout.

HUMANNEQUINS

All is not what it seems in the Howard's
Department Store window display.

CHARACTERS

M1, Mannequin 1

M2, Mannequin 2

CAZ, an ex-soldier

JAN, an onlooker

SARAH, an insomniac

AUTHOR'S NOTE

*All characters could be played by any gender.
Alternative names are:*

TOM, an ex-soldier

JON, an onlooker

SIMON, an insomniac

SCENE:

Music is playing: 'This Time Tomorrow' by Brandi Carlile.

The stage is set with several dressed mannequins, representing a shop window display positioned down stage left, at a slight angle. Mannequin 1 sits crossed legged on a wicker chair at the front of the group, holding up a large, old, local newspaper which is positioned so that the audience are unable to see their face. A life-size, ceramic statue of a dog is positioned at their feet. Mannequin 2 stands facing away from the audience and could be partly hidden to prevent detection. Both are still and silent whilst the audience enter the auditorium. The lighting should suggest that it is nighttime with the window area lit with artificial lighting.

Mannequin 1 lowers the newspaper slowly. They speak authoritatively but in a slightly detached manner. Parts of the speech are clearly quoted from their newspaper.

M1 (*Addressing the audience*) Have you ever looked at a shop window display and noticed the mannequins? Have you ever wondered why they are all different, why we are so different? As a young child, I remember running past the window of Howard's department store in the high street as quickly as I could in case the "pointy ladies" got me. (*Laughing*) Once, when I plucked up the courage to stop and look at them, I was sure that one of them winked at me. Everyone said I was making up stories. But I knew what I had seen. In the December of 1984, Howard's Department Store on the city high street was awarded the first prize by the Weekly Gazette for its (*reading*) "innovative Christmas window display" which included five exceptionally life-like mannequins dressed as if at a Christmas party, cleverly surrounded by a range of seasonal products available to purchase from the department store. It was estimated that "over seven thousand people specifically came to see the visual wonder which delighted young and old due to its creative charm". For the six weeks running up to New Year's Day, visitors from far and wide came to look at the window. Several of those who visited more than once, were surprised to see that the number of mannequins in the display appeared to grow, but they dismissed their observations as incorrect, attributed it to one too many Christmas tipples or simply questioned their sanity. (*laughing*) Most noticed nothing. (*Turning to another mannequin*) That was when you joined us wasn't it? Escaping an abusive relationship, seeking peace.

M2 (*moves to stand next* **M1***, to the audience*). Hmm. (*reflecting*) That Christmas night my partner had become so violent that I ran out of the house, not having a clue where to go. The abuse had gone on for years but was getting worse. I had been put in hospital twice by then and everyone was quick to advise me to leave, but not actually how to do it. He had punched me in the face so hard that my jaw was hanging loose like a broken puppet. I knew that next time he would kill me. I literally ran for my life and found myself staring through my swollen eyes, gazing at the party scene wishing that I could join you, safe and sound, away from his punishing beatings. And I did.

M1 *puts their hand out to* **M2** *and they hold onto each other affectionately.*

At that point, there is a kerfuffle at the back of the theatre (or somewhere in the auditorium) as **CAZ** *crashes noisily through the door. She is carrying her worldly goods (bag of clothes, sleeping bag etc) on her back and carries a half empty whisky bottle in one hand and a rope (which acted as a dog lead) in another. She is clearly very drunk but not aggressive. She clumsily makes his way through the audience and up onto the stage.*

M2 Here is Caz.

M1 (*to* **M2**) This may be our last night to save her. I don't think she has many more nights left in her.

M2 I thought she would come in once Bess had come to us.

M1 But animals are better at knowing when their time has come. She knew that she couldn't survive another cold night of wandering the city with her. She knew she needed to rest.

M2 Let's try with Caz. She has walked by every night since Bess left her, perhaps she knows.

M1 (*to the audience*) Some people are understandably freaked out when they realise that we are somehow alive but many of those whom we see at night experience so much confusion and chaos in their lives that living mannequins are just another aspect of life that is impossible to make sense of, and they are the most accepting. Many already have distorted perceptions of the world, this is just one more. Some need to talk, some need someone to listen but most just need to rest.

By now, **CAZ** *is on stage. She is looking into the shop window, she has quietened now, transfixed by the ceramic dog that is by the feet of* **M1**.

When **CAZ** *arrives* **M1** *and* **M2** *have adopted the poses as mannequins again.*

JAN *appears from the wings at the right side of the stage and stands quietly listening.*

CAZ Well, that certainly looks like Bess. Is that you, girl?

M1 Yes Caz, it is.

CAZ I lost her. Why is she with you? Is she dead?

M2 No, just resting. She needed to rest, Caz. She wanted to be able to just sit and watch the world go by from the warmth of the shop window. Wouldn't you like that? To rest.

CAZ Yes.

M1 Come and be with us, Caz. Come and rest with Bess.

CAZ I can't.

M2 Why not?

CAZ Because… (*she starts to look down and shake and sob quietly*)

M1 (*to audience*) Caz was once a soldier.

CAZ (*looking up*) Part of the British army.

M1 Now Caz wanders the streets. Night after night.
CAZ I can't be inside. I have to be able to get out.
(*She starts to sob again*)

M2 I want to comfort her.

M1 You know we cannot leave the window.

M2 Yes—but it's so hard to watch.

M1 I know.

M2 Caz, please. You need to rest. You haven't got long now. Please join us.

CAZ I can't be inside. Not since…

M1 I know. (*to audience*) Twenty two years ago, members of Caz's battalion, a group of UN peacekeepers, were drinking in a local bar after a day spent helping local people build a pumping unit to enable them to access clean water. They had been deployed in that region for over six months and generally enjoyed an excellent relationship with the community whom they had helped to re-build a number of houses, a school and a cottage hospital which had been destroyed over the previous decade of fighting and destruction.

CAZ We had been helping them. They liked us.

M1 Most did. But not everyone appreciated the presence of foreign soldiers. The building in which they were celebrating a birthday was blown to pieces by a bomb, which caused the two-storey building to crumble and those inside to be crushed under the rubble. Caz and one other were the only survivors from nearly eighty people. She waited over 48 hours to be removed from the rubble.

CAZ I thought I was going to die. It was like being in a tomb. Alive in a tomb. The weight of the building was pinning me down and my mouth, my eyes and my nose were full of dust. I couldn't breathe but I stayed alive. For hours and hours all I could hear were the moans and screams of the others and then silence. I waited to die but I didn't. They died. I wanted to die. Every night I relive it, every night I fear being trapped and I have to walk. Have to be outside.

M2 Come to us, Caz. You'd be safe here.

CAZ (*emphatically*) I can't be inside.

CAZ *starts to go, but then turns back.*

CAZ Can I, can I give something to Bess?

M1 *and* **M2** *look at each other.*

M2 Let's try. We haven't done it before, but we might be able to.

M1 What is it?

CAZ It's her rope. It has joined us for 7 years and I want her to remember me.

M2 She won't forget you, Caz. You fed her and kept her safe. She loves you.

CAZ*: (starting to sob again)* And I love her. For so many years she's been my only friend.

She puts up her hand holding the rope to the window. At this point **M1** *reaches out their hand and takes the rope. At the point that the rope passes through the imaginary glass, there should be a moment of resistance. When the rope is with* **M1***, they can put the rope by Bess before patting her.*

CAZ (*to* **M1** *and* **M2**) Thank you. (*to Bess*) Thank you.

M2 Goodbye Caz.

*As she gathers her things, she takes a very large
swig out of the whisky bottle, starts to sing
quietly to herself and exits stage right.*

M1 (*to audience*) Caz's body will be found in the
doorway of the town hall buildings. Disgruntled
council workers will complain about the heap of
rubbish blocking their way into work that
morning until one realises that the pile of dirty
clothes and baggage is actually a person. A dead
person. They will be momentarily shocked and
disgusted and then will return to their daily
routines.

At this point, **JAN** *at the side of the stage comes
forward to address* **M1** *and* **M2**.

JAN I want to join you.

M1 *and* **M2** *remain still and silent.*

JAN I know what you are up to. If you don't let
me, I will tell people. The police. I'll tell the
police. I need to join you. (*with increasing
desperation and aggression*) My life is shit. A
clichéd pile of shit. My husband is having an
affair with his PA, I hate my fucking job and I
can't afford to pay the mortgage or the bills. Let
me join you.

Pause

I want to join you. I want to get away from all of this. (*Sitting down in despair with her head in her hands*)

Pause

M1 That's not what we are here for.

JAN (*looking up*) Please! My life is a fucking mess.

M2 But you still have hope.

JAN Do I?

M2 Yes. Your life is a mess, but you have choices. Things could get better.

M1 We are here for those who have no choice. Who need to escape. Who need to rest.

JAN But I do need to escape. My life is a pile of crap.

Beat

So, how did you get to be there then?

M1 I have…had…a condition. I am…was a physical empath.

JAN What is that?

M1 I was so sensitive to others, so empathetic, that I suffered the pain and illnesses of those around me.

JAN I've never heard of that.

M1 I don't think it's that unusual, except my version was extreme. As a child I would experience the symptoms of friends and family, such as headaches or nausea but it became so much worse after puberty. When my friend at college developed cancer and was undergoing chemotherapy, I also suffered their side-effects of the treatment—I spent three months vomiting, my skin became sore and blistered and I lost much of my hair. The doctors tested me and found nothing wrong. When my brother broke his leg in a go-karting accident, I experienced severe pain in my leg for many months and had to use crutches to walk. Again, medical experts found nothing. My family and friends became sceptical and felt I was just seeking attention. No one understood. When my grandmother was diagnosed with dementia and I realised that I too had started to suffer from some memory loss and confusion, I knew that I couldn't continue and that's when I decided to end it all. I had to do it whilst I was able to think for myself. I'd become estranged from my family and friends, and I just couldn't face any more. I intended to throw myself off the bridge. So, I drank a whole bottle of brandy and I set off to the river. But the brandy had been too much, and I had to stop to be sick. I was standing next to the window, here, leaning against it as I was throwing up… and I simply fell through.

JAN But how? I don't understand.

M1 I don't know. The glass seemed to melt away and I found myself inside the window. Looking out, but suddenly feeling calm and well and clear headed.

JAN Did it cure you? Did you stop suffering?

M1 In a way. I stopped experiencing any shared pain or the debilitating symptoms of others and, for the first time ever, enjoyed the feeling of detachment and the ability to view the world with objectivity.

JAN I want to stop suffering too.

Beat

So what exactly are you?

M2 We are humannequins, no longer a human like you, but not dead either. And, when we wish, when the time is right, we can choose to stop living altogether and become inanimate. You can see that was the choice made by several here.

JAN So, why don't more people know about you?

M2   There are many aspects of life that humans don't really understand, and they choose to ignore. So many people are helped in many ways by different and unlikely things. This is just one more.

M1 As we have said, you have choices. Get a divorce. Change your job. Sell your house. You are still able to take control.

JAN I haven't got the energy.

M2 You have—you just need to find it.

SARAH *is sitting near the stage in the audience and has been scrolling on her phone and becoming increasing agitated throughout this exchange. She stands up she is highly agitated and upset.*

SARAH (*shouts out in frustration*) Why can't I ever fucking sleep?

M1 Now, she needs our help.

SARAH I can't sleep. Why can't I sleep. Month after month, I haven't had a proper sleep. Can't get to sleep. Wake up in the night. Exhausted in the day. Can't sleep.

M2 I think she might have had enough. She's been walking every night for months now.

> **SARAH** *grabs her coat and walks onto the stage. She stares into the window, remaining highly agitated.*

SARAH (*suddenly noticing* **JAN** *standing behind her*) And what the fuck are you doing there, standing in the shadows. What's your fucking problem?

JAN I was…

SARAH Don't try to fucking explain, I'm not interested. I'm past fucking caring. I just can't sleep. I can't stand this any longer. I can't do this anymore. I need to sleep!

M1 (*reaching out*) Take my hand.

M2 Come to us. Rest with us now.

SARAH Yes, I want to rest. I need to rest. But what… who are you?

M1 We are here to help you rest.

M2 (*to* **JAN**): Go and find the energy you need to sort out your life. Change things for the better, you can do that. You can still help yourself and make choices.

JAN (*realising she has options*) Yes, I will try. I think I understand now. Thank you!

M2 We will always be here for you, if you really need us.

JAN Yes. Thank you!

> **JAN** *steps away and watches as* **SARAH** *holds out both her hands.* **M1** *and* **M2** *take a hand each and guide her into the window. As she passes through the imaginary glass she visibly relaxes and becomes silent and calm. She then becomes part of the mannequin scene as* **JAN** *looks on. They all stand still in silence for several seconds.*

> *Sharp blackout.*

> *Music: 'Changes' by Langhorne Slim*

HERE COMES THE SUN

As Gemma awaits the results from her pregnancy test, she is joined by Margaret, a friend from the past, whose kindness Gemma has never forgotten. Together they recall happy memories and some of lessons that Gemma learned, which she may find particularly useful to remember today.

HERE COMES THE SUN was shortlisted for the Chesil Theatre TakeTen New Writing Festival, 2023.

CHARACTERS

GEMMA, a female of around 40 years old

MARGARET, an older woman

AUTHOR'S NOTE

** In order to heighten the anticipation of the result,
two identical pregnancy test sticks should be
available, and the actor playing the part of*
GEMMA *should take one as she walks on stage,*
without *knowing the result.*

SCENE:

A kitchen table with two chairs, centre stage. Downstage stage left, is a pile of bags including a work laptop case and a handbag containing a mobile phone. They appear to have been thrown there in a hurry. A mug of hot tea has been left on the table. A toilet flushes off stage and **GEMMA** *enters from stage left doing up the flies on her trousers. She is carrying a pregnancy testing stick* which she places on the table face down so that she cannot see the result.*

She picks up a mug of tea which she holds with both hands, as if warming her hands. She moves downstage. She takes a sip of the tea and stares into space. A pause. **MARGARET** *enters the stage from stage right. She is old, wears a baggy cardigan and slippers. She is carrying a pile of old board games. She carefully places the boxes on the kitchen table and sits down.*

MARGARET *(gesturing towards the pile of games)* I don't suppose that you want to…?

GEMMA *(realising that she is there)* What? No thanks. Not now. Just waiting.

MARGARET Waiting?

GEMMA For the result *(indicates the pregnancy test on the table)*. They don't take long. Actually, I think they are too quick—I need more time.

MARGARET Oh?

GEMMA Time to appreciate this moment of blissful ignorance. Before I know one way or another how my life might change. Or not.

MARGARET I see.

Silence

Do you remember our games?

GEMMA Of course, I do—that's why you are here, again.

MARGARET True.

GEMMA Every Saturday for almost two years, Mum would dump me at your house for a couple of hours.

MARGARET She was trying to earn some extra money working at the supermarket. You enjoyed our afternoons together, didn't you?

GEMMA They were the best. You were the only one that ever had the time for me. To talk and to listen. You never seemed to judge me or be annoyed by my questions or be angry like she was.

MARGARET Well, your mother was busy and did always seem to be rushing somewhere. I was retired and had the time. And Henry hadn't long died, so I was lonely.

GEMMA So was I. *(She sits at the table next to* **MARGARET***)*

MARGARET Do you remember, for the first couple of months I let you choose what you wanted to play and every time you chose Scrabble.

GEMMA I liked Scrabble. I thought it could be won by skill—it wasn't just due to chance.

MARGARET Really? The letters you pick up are not in your control.

GEMMA But you could get tactical and inventive, and I liked that. Although your Scrabble dictionary prevented some of my most creative words…. And you never let me win!

MARGARET What would you have learned from that? That would have been pointless. I wanted you to find out about yourself. About life. Henry hated board games, so we didn't often play them. He always said that they should have been spelt B-O-R-E-D games! But I loved them. As a retired teacher I could see that each one could be used to teach something about real life.

GEMMA (*smiling*) Well, our games of Scrabble certainly taught me not to assume that a sweet little old lady was going to be nice and throw the game!

MARGARET Never! And to hold onto the good stuff and to wait for the right time? To make the best of what you have.

GEMMA I guess so.

MARGARET What about draughts, what did that teach you?

GEMMA To choose a better game!

MARGARET I agree! Just dreadful! But in the end, Snakes and Ladders was our favourite, wasn't it? The best one for helping you to learn and prepare for life.

GEMMA Yes. At first, I used to hate the lack of control, the outcome was purely down to luck— all at the roll of a dice.

MARGARET Die.

GEMMA (*surprised*) Sorry?

MARGARET The roll of a die. There's only one!

GEMMA (*laughing*) Always teaching!

MARGARET (*laughing*) Sorry—that's who I am. Was.

Beat

You used to become so upset and angry when you landed on a snake.

GEMMA I hated it. It was just so unfair!

MARGARET Well, you know what they say…life isn't fair!

GEMMA (*joining in*) Life isn't fair! It used to eat me up, the injustice of landing on a snake, particularly that big one, just as I thought I was going to win! I wanted to cry!

MARGARET I think you did cry once!

GEMMA Yes, I remember.

Beat

But it wasn't the game that made me sad and angry and frustrated, it was my life. The lack of control as a child, relying on adults for everything. Relying on my mother. Dealing with her chaotic decisions and poor choices. Even at that age it felt unbearable.

Beat

But you listened to my fears and worries and didn't dismiss me as a stupid little child. And once you had explained to me that the game was a metaphor for life and we talked about how to laugh at the ridiculousness of it all sometimes, I started to understand that it's all about how you deal with the snakes and ladders, and it became fun!

MARGARET Why do you think that so many cultures have their own versions of the game? People across the world trying to make sense of their lives using a board game? Some cultures have made the snakes and ladders about sins and virtues, put a religious twist on it, but I think that the concept of luck is more appropriate.

Silence

GEMMA I did appreciate our time together. The effort you made to make me feel welcome. I was just your neighbour, the sullen little girl from next door.

MARGARET You were quiet and shy, but not sullen.

GEMMA That's what I had been told.

MARGARET But after a while you seemed to become so much more happy. Sunnier.

GEMMA I did feel happier.

Beat

And letting me borrow your books was wonderful—my very own private library.

MARGARET They were just sitting there, collecting dust on the shelf. I was glad someone was reading them again and it was fun for us to discuss them.

GEMMA Those chats, the games, the Earl Grey tea!

MARGARET You had never tasted that before, I wasn't sure you liked it?

GEMMA I did. Once I'd got used to it! Since then, I can't drink anything else! And the wonderful homemade ginger biscuits! Delicious…had to be dunked though!

MARGARET Definitely best dunked in tea.

GEMMA If you wanted to keep your fillings!

Beat

I wish I'd got the recipe from you.

MARGARET It was a secret. But I would have told you…if you'd asked.

GEMMA I should have. You would probably have even taught me how to make them…if I'd asked.

MARGARET I would have done.

GEMMA And then, out of the blue, you went and died!

MARGARET Yes. Sorry. I was very old, but no one had expected it, particularly not me. When I went to bed that night, I thought I just had a nasty bout of indigestion. Not a bad way to go. For me.

GEMMA But it was such a horrible shock for me! And she didn't let me go to your funeral. Said I was too young, that I wouldn't understand what was happening. I never had the chance to say goodbye.

MARGARET Your mother probably thought she was doing the right thing.

GEMMA Did she? Did she ever really think about anything? It was always the easiest option with her. It was always about her. And we moved house soon after and that part of my life ended. I hadn't realised how special our time had been, until it was all over. She's the main reason we left it so late to start trying for a baby. I couldn't bring myself to repeat the same mistakes. I've worried that bad parenting may be in my genes. I didn't want any child to feel like it was an inconvenience, unwanted, nothing more than a nuisance. Dev wanted a baby so much but said he would wait until the time felt right for me too. And when I eventually got my head in the right place and we decided to try, we both assumed it would just happen, but it didn't. And now we have run out of time for more IVF treatment. Too old. To be honest, we couldn't cope with anymore. So much disappointment and sadness. I couldn't have kept going for so long if it hadn't been for our afternoons together, remembering the need to keep hoping. Eventually, it just became too much to deal with. Ridiculous but not at all funny. Too many snakes and not enough ladders! But once we'd officially given up and we had given notice at our jobs and were planning our travels, we relaxed and started having sex again. Proper lovemaking not the "made to order", "quick, fuck me while I'm fertile" type of sex. (*looking quickly to* **MARGARET**) Sorry! And last week I realised that my period hadn't come, so… (*tailing off, looking back to the pregnancy testing stick*). I had to do the test before Dev came back. I need to know so that I can be strong for him again. If I have to be.

MARGARET You were always very thoughtful. (*She puts her hand on* **GEMMA**'s *arm*) It seems to me that society has always been obsessed with women and girls having children too early or when they weren't married. Obviously, many lives have been devastated by unwanted pregnancies but I have often worried that so many people could have regrets when they realise that they've missed their time in life to have a child. That their opportunity had passed, and they had almost forgotten to have children.

GEMMA Did that happen to you?

MARGARET In a way. I met Henry later in life, it was already too late for children by then. Because I had been a primary school teacher for so many years, I had educated and nurtured hundreds, possibly thousands of young lives. That had to be enough, I had no choice.

Beat

But our afternoons together really meant so much to me.

GEMMA Me too. A special connection! (*putting her hand on top of* **MARGARET***'s and taking a deep breath*) So, is it going to be another long, grim slide down a snake or a rapid, joyful climb up that giant ladder on the board of life?

MARGARET (*taking* **GEMMA***'s hand and holding it reassuringly in both of her hands*) Whatever happens, remember that a ladder is only a roll of a die away.

GEMMA*'s mobile phone rings. She jumps up out of her chair, moves to the pile of bags, fumbling around, she takes her phone out of her handbag and looks at it.*

GEMMA It's Dev! (*She returns to the table and turns over the pregnancy test to check the result before answering the call. She waits a moment to take in the result).*

Either: If the pregnancy test result is negative:

GEMMA (*moving downstage as she talks*) Hi darling, how are you?... Good… Are you still at work?... No, I'm at home. Came back early cos I wasn't feeling too good… just had a bit of a headache, that's all… Don't worry, I'm okay…. Yes, really, I'm fine. It'll be gone soon, I'm sure. Hey, I was just looking at the itinerary the travel company sent through today, did you see it? I can't wait to get away from this cold weather and catch some rays! The Great Barrier Reef looks amazing, doesn't it? Can't wait. It's going to be such fun!…When will you be back?…Oh, okay….Only more week of work to go...Yes, that's a good idea, I really don't fancy cooking this evening! Sure. See you then…Love you too! (*She ends the call*) Oh well, I've always wanted to visit Australia.

MARGARET Remember, there will be another ladder. (*She gathers the games and stands up by the table*)

GEMMA (*turning round to her and smiling*) Always!

Music starts to play: Nina Simone's "Here Comes the Sun".

Lights fade.

Or: If the pregnancy test result is positive:

GEMMA (*moving downstage as she talks*) Hi darling, how are you?...Yes, I'm fine. I had a headache, but it's gone already… Really. Hey, Dev, any chance you could skip off work early tonight? There's something I want to tell you… Yes, everything's fine… Better than fine, but we may have to make a few adjustments to our plans… I can't tell you over the phone… So, when will you be back?… Great! See you very soon then… Love you too! (*She ends the call*). I think I'd better cancel that trip.

MARGARET (*smiling and gathering the games*) I'm so pleased. You will be an excellent mother. Goodbye, Gemma.

MARGARET *exits stage right.*

GEMMA Goodbye, Margaret.

Music starts to play: Nina Simone's "Here Comes the Sun".

Lights fade to black.

Printed in Great Britain
by Amazon